Walserian Waltzes

Also by Gad Hollander:
The smallness of it all
Page
Video Residua (Orphic)
Figures of Speech
Sleep, Memory
The Palaver (with images by Andrew Bick)

FILMS:
Mnemosyne
Background Music (Orphic)
Euripides' Movies
Diary of a Sane Man

AUDIO:
The Palaver (CD)

Walserian Waltzes

Gad Hollander

Avec Books
Penngrove

Grateful acknowledgment is made to the editors of the following publications in which parts of this work previously appeared: *An Avec Sampler Two, Central Park, First Intensity, Kater Murr's Press and Stride.*

ISBN: 1-880713-21-7

Library of Congress

Catalog Card Number: 99-73733

This book was produced with a generous grant from The Fund for Poetry, a contribution from Peter Straub and an anonymous contribution.

Cover art by Andrew Bick

Cover design by Colleen Barclay

First Edition

Avec Books
P.O. Box 1059
Penngrove, CA 94951

in memory of my father

One can only think horizontally.

o

To be in harmony with the universe is to fall into wisdom. It means that you know everything, are in agreement with everything, but not with much else!

o

I imagine man's isolation thus: a wintry landscape in which the snow is like materialized ingenuity; a light mist blurring the contours of the land; white silence, and in it, Man, ghost-like, an exile among the snow flakes.

—E.M. Cioran

Robert had a thought and sat down. He had already been seated a few moments earlier, before rising to stretch his legs. He was about to dance a brief waltz when the thought fell into his head. So he sat down to ponder it. He did not write it down. He did not put ink to paper as was his habit with thoughts. It was not that kind of thought. It could not be put into writing, could not be sung or painted or turned into a meaningful action. It was the kind of thought he classified as pure – of and for itself, inconsequential and alone, a little out of this world. So he sat down, as if under or beside his thought, and reflected on how it resisted his scrutiny, how it defied his application, how it held fast to its own integrity. And it could not be ignored, this thought, could not be dumped on the scrapheap of all his thoughts and simply be forgotten. It had to be preserved. So he carried it around like a page (albeit a blank page) which fluttered or billowed or rustled in his mind from time to time, evoking images from the past – a woman, a sailboat, a picnic. The experience of this incommunicable thought pleased and disturbed Robert simultaneously. On the one hand it seemed as if it had fallen into his head at just the right moment in his life, clarifying and making sense of everything. He knew that it was no illusion, that it was a real thought which had to be treated seriously and with respect. In adopting this attitude he felt that he was being loyal to himself, since he had always been satisfied to be himself and this sort of habitual reflexivity suited him and was a trademark of his character. But in fact he was only following a primitive inclination to sit down and do nothing, not even wait. So while he was pleased to be himself, to be Robert Walser, the Swiss writer, he was also disturbed by it – just as the Swiss writer Robert Walser would have been both pleased and disturbed (he thought) to be not only himself but another Robert Walser who happened to be a Swiss writer. But Robert could not be absolutely sure if there really was another Robert Walser. He toyed with the word *really* in his mind till its meaning blurred and faded like an old charcoal drawing. His thought had produced a configuration of pleasure and pain which reflected his delicate state of mind and cloaked itself in a mysterious light. So he sat down and pondered it. He was not Swiss, he had never been to Switzerland, though he was inclined to be neutral, even a bit aloof at times, and had always loved the mountains. And yet it was not these uncanny resemblances that seized his mind now – even if he *was* in his seventies, *had* dropped dead in the snow and *did* lose his hat in the process – but the disquieting evidence of a duplicate existence in an identical but distinctly separate body which he could not countenance as his own. Everything seemed to be exactly the same – the scene, the action, the light – as if Robert Walser were re-enacting his own death. Clearly that was impossible. Even if a particular fleeting gesture or expression was repeated and rendered identical, the truth of Robert Walser and his act of dying could never have been reconstituted. I can only speculate as to the nature of these facts from within the realm of possibilities. The snow and the corpse lying in it are both equally cold, life-size renditions and perfect models of the man, the place and the event. For my part I only know which is living, which dead – who fell, and why.

The madness business introduced itself into Robert's head like a gift. Robert suspected that something was amiss and wondered what menacing hand lay behind it. Born into the latter part of the last century, he wrote novels, stories and odd prose pieces well into the first part of this century. As many of his writings were published as not and were variously described as poetic, laconic, good, bad. Those who described also judged – reviewing, dismissing or ignoring his texts with the sarcasm of blisters on a corpse's tongue. Robert bore derision across the expanse of his brow with the equanimity of sails gliding across a lake. In his own lifetime the verdicts pronounced upon his writings had little effect on his mind or his body – yet I find this hard to believe, even if the obverse was true too. He began at the end, with a random circular thought inside his head, first informing, then colluding with the madness business outside it. He attributed the madness business firstly to his obsession with writing and secondly to his compulsion to be mad. His obsession and compulsion thus kept a tab on each other in a system of checks and balances which prevented his relapse into total sanity or total madness. It was a kind of gift, this system, a promotional marketing ploy of the time distributed like free perfume to passersby in the street. The gift came wrapped in silk tissues and no genius has been given the hands to deflect it. Robert dreamed of ribboned snowflakes laced in the shape of his body. He was a waiter. Before dying he wanted to serve, to bring this or that – a cup of tea or coffee – to one or another of his readers, always observing his own civility. Balancing a cup and saucer in his hand, he walked from one end of the cosmos to the other. Once he went so far as to pick a coffee bean from a plant that grew by the way, wanting to place it decoratively beside the teaspoon. As his hand reached out to pick it from a cluster hanging on a stalk, the bean momentarily eclipsed the sun, its shadow briefly obscuring the dirt under his fingernails. At that instant Robert felt purified, glimpsing his own mortality in the fruit. Thereafter his shadow moved lithely on the floor of the world, like the shadow of a fish. The event was recounted as a miracle. Death and decorum soon became his playmates. He developed a desire to inculcate a civil mode of behaviour in our feeding habits. He wanted to invest the crude sounds, odours and gestures of mastication, digestion and defecation in an epic of functionality informed by the body's nourishment business. He would attend to all that shit with humility and grace, preserving a semblance of order within the complexities of his internal body. The madness business only entered his head as a belated distraction. He began to imagine that a circus had pitched its tent under his eyelids, and whilst he was seduced by its strange enchantment, the dull monotony of the band-music soon grew irksome. He took to drinking spring water but failed to flush out the noise. As he was about to die and abnegate all responsibilities that life had foisted upon him, he suddenly realised his oldest ambition – to improvise dying – and remembered to say to himself, loudly and clearly, what he had neglected to say all his life: *Jesus, Robert! Be lucid!* Then he went on dying, as usual, with a strange fulfilment in the air around him. This myth was invented and recorded by a writer in his dream, one in a series whirring madly in the round, attached to no-one.

At dawn he wondered why he bothered bothering the world with re-arrangements of notes. He recalled his folly upon waking and a sharp discomfort pierced his eyelids. His visions aborted, old notebooks became receptacles of silence, their notes lost, misremembered in the fog of origins. Yet some survived, encoded in miraculous syntax, like homing signals from abandoned worlds. A note on thought as action resonated briefly over the valley, then sank out of earshot. Doctors who have long ago vanished from the valley, and others who have surrendered the heights, would have called it Depression. No-one knows where they've disappeared to, so many brilliant, dazzling beings. Their sanatoriums were filmed in black and white: eyes white and lashes black, hearts and fingernails bent whitewards in a sanctified cleansing rite performed with faint pulsebeats and white dreams lapping the Alpine air. The writer under such conditions profoundly relaxes his ear. His deafness rolls across the page in a wash of greys. He is afraid and has my sympathy. He looks out of the window in a desperate gaze of distraction: mountains and memory lull him towards sleep. He succumbs, then reawakens to the sound of notes hammering out dead adages (*always darkest before dawn*) or vain psychological memos (*leave self-expression out of things when self and things are discrete units*). Such hopeful counsel proves ineffectual as he picks up his pen and weeps. Over lunch he swallows and ponders his own tears. *I think I've written this scene before, but I'll write it once again.* A second writing, given to a second reader, so like the first, given to the first reader. From exile to exile, it is his way of moving in a landscape towards moonlight, following dusk and the drudgery of day; a way of staving off the self's intrusive dance-steps on the page. I have attempted a description of a writer at his table, without regard for the table he bends over or the chair he sits on. These things in themselves, he says, make their own pretty picture.

Robert had a thought and sat down. The thought had recurred throughout his life, assuming an abstract shape, and now, at the moment of his death, was no different. Though it helped to map the limits of his life, it had nothing to do with his death. Aware of its last rite in his brain, Robert sat down in the company of his thought. It happened in the mountains, in winter, when the mountains are covered with snow. It was a thought he had always known, a shadowy trace moving inside his head like a sandwich-board figure without a message. It clung inside him as he sat down, as if to guide him on his final journey. Meanwhile the snow that covered the mountains was light. And it was almost a swoon, the way Robert sat down, the way his body descended ponderously, as if the thought had occurred in order to prevent him from falling. While nearby a woman settled briefly on a bench, her body awkwardly hunched to encompass the baby in her arms. It was colder and windier there, fifty yards up the slope, and it may have been the fragile image of mother and child in the winter landscape that made Robert nearly faint with compassion. He sat down on the ground and watched the young woman as she eased her baby's hunger before resuming her trek over the hilltop. Bounded by a circular horizon, her pantomime seemed so close he could almost touch it, take part in it. But as he reached out he toppled backwards into the snow and died. His hat rolled a few feet away from his head, and his face took on a frozen expression that gave him the appearance of being not seriously dead. Yet Robert was somehow reassured that he was at last truly dead.

Like the thought which came and accompanied him into death, such reassurance left him dizzy, perplexed, as if he had suddenly stepped out of character, along with the rest of the world, or as if he and the world had invented and eliminated gravity in a random gesture. Robert was in his seventies, after all, and knew the difference between word and flesh, and he gave no religious credence to dying. Nevertheless, when an angel drifted by, smiling, he returned the greeting cordially, despite his own surprise. For he would have expected that angelic demeanour to be more confrontational, even brutal, certainly less guided by the circumspections of polite society. Yet on seeing the angel smile, and lost for words to say how his own impeccable manners remained intact, Robert smiled back: the simple, transmuted smile of a corpse.

With a different name, he stood on a streetcorner calling to himself by name – then paused, wondering why he was doing it. He remembered that he'd wanted to talk to himself, so he called again and gained his attention. He was not mad. He wanted to conduct a decent conversation but knew that he could not rely on anyone to speak to him as he would speak to them. He wanted to talk about names and their permanent attachment to people, but he felt handicapped by the strangeness of his own name and concerned about the restless nature of his soul. He wondered if there was a causal relationship between his uneasy name and his unquiet soul or if these merely coincided by chance. Over the years his name and everything that went with it had lain awash in its own quietus, like a stone on a beach, while his soul had moved to and fro ceaselessly like a wave. How, he asked, could the same wave strike incessantly at exactly the same spot? And was it always the same wave crashing or only the infinite parts of a much larger but finite entity? Although he loved to meander aimlessly in his thoughts and was in the habit of talking to himself, he did not often call to himself by name, and it was this sudden familiarity with himself that troubled him. He believed in maintaining a certain standard of decorum, even within the exclusive privacy of his self. He was capable of conducting a perfectly sober dialogue with himself, shifting his attention between words and silences simply by speaking and listening in turn, but his aim was always to resolve such conversations with an idea, or the germ of an idea, and whenever he succeeded in this ambition he would refer to the event as 'a fruitful conversation'. He was interested in the numinous constructions that propped up the silences around his talk rather than in the palpability of his words, for he believed that that was where ideas were sown and later nurtured. Yet the paradox of this process – namely, that a fully developed idea could not re-invent its primary thought, its original formulation – completely escaped him. That is why he stood on the streetcorner and called to himself. He wanted to remind himself of this quirky anomaly in his thought process, but as soon as he acknowledged his calling to himself he forgot what he had wanted to say. To passers-by in the street he was known as the bird, for he would flap his arms about whenever he called himself, shouting: I'm a bird, I'm a bird! For them the idea was precisely the word.

Robert's obsessive affair with failure was no pushover job but hard work. So many nights and days consumed bemoaning his fate, tear-drenched sleepless nights pondering the impossible, dark days wandering wistfully through the streets, shying from old and new acquaintances alike, mornings and evenings sunk in heart-wrenching rituals of despair and protracted meditations on nothing. No part of his psyche was safe from his thoughts, nor could any single thought survive the assaults of his mind. It was a dead-end and he had a bad time of it, that much was obvious. Yet to express it so curtly fails to impress the sinister nature of time's machinations — an idea which Robert found more interesting than despair per se, one that he'd cultivate during short-lived optimistic cycles. Time, failure, success. From these he would make a compost to fertilise death, less for posterity's sake than for his own modest ambition to gain credentials in some hypothetical afterlife. Like a penitent lusting at the foot of a shrine, Robert looked up the word failure, examined it, and found its Latin source: *fallere*, to deceive, be concealed from, escape observation, be ignorant of, probably related to Greek *phelos*, deceitful, to Sanskrit *hrunati*, he gets lost, and to Old Slavic *zulu*, bad, evil. Although the connections escaped him, he sensed salvation forging towards him through failure's clumsy syllables, as if the word, propped up by its etymology, cried out like a babe in the arms of a priest, who intones melodically: I have not forsaken you, you are deceived and concealed, you escape observation, you are ignored, you will be lost, you are bad and evil, you will crown the underside of the world like a worm. And by nightfall, swathed in the pages of dictionaries, he fell asleep, clasping his pain until dawn.

Write, said Robert therapeutically to himself, but don't mention your problems. Write about the dawn or grazing sheep or bulldozers scraping a new road. Anything. Just write and get the sickness business out of your head. But Robert refused to listen to himself and went out instead. He thought he could empty the sickness business from his head, thought he could dump it out of sight like garbage. He stood on the corner of a busy junction and watched the traffic flowing in contrary directions. He noticed how the volume was greater in one direction than the other and, as the hours passed, how it decreased, then levelled out in all directions. Though the junction occupied several roads, most of the traffic flowed along one of two main routes, and as the volume increased again towards evening he noticed that it was heavier in the direction which was lighter at the start of the day. Robert stood at the corner for five consecutive days. He saw that the pattern was the same every day: heavy traffic in one direction in the morning, then a lull, a levelling out, and finally heavy traffic in the opposite direction in the evening. The experience taught him about that daily occurrence known as the rush hour, when people hurry to and from work in the mornings and evenings. He could not understand why they rushed at all, one way or the other, especially as they moved more slowly and laboriously during those times of the day than at other times. Yet on the basis of his experience he applied for a job as a traffic warden, but failed to get an interview. A friend reminded him that jobs were at a premium, and a man in his seventies who listed "watching traffic" as a hobby would be unlikely to qualify for any sort of job. It was the nearest anyone had ever told him to his face that he was totally unsuitable for the job. With hindsight he realised that he should never have mentioned anything about his hobbies in his application letter. Yet it wasn't whim that made him go out to study the traffic but the advice of that same friend, who had insisted that he must confront the real world if he wanted to get the sickness business out of his head. But Robert had always found the real world tedious, and his prejudice was only reinforced after watching the traffic for days on end. Having survived his five-day stint with reality, he rushed home to the comfort of the sickness business in his head. As he nursed his madness he realised that something was not right in his head if he could just stand there watching the traffic, not even counting the cars or spotting the occasional rarity, just riveted dumbly like an angel guarding the rivers of Paradise. He sat down and wrote a letter to his friend, describing his experience in detail and questioning the friend's judgement. He reflected endlessly and profoundly on his recent experience but failed to send the letter. Indeed it could not be sent because Robert is still writing it. It remains an unfinished letter which has by now become a therapeutic process, a scribbling forth. I'm able to judge his writing from his prolonged silence, a more vibrant and pronounced silence than the one I'd grown accustomed to before he went to and returned from the real world; a torpid silence in which I can hear my own thoughts adrift in distant spaces – fluid thoughts unable to anchor themselves in any articulate sounds, let alone the mad syllabics of his letter.

I am sitting on the inside of a madhouse. An opera is performed in the background, the foreground, the ground between. The mad weep quietly to themselves. They settle in their seats as if at home, in their own town, their own country, their own part of the world, with claims to sanctity as well as sanity. But this is only a madhouse. Like the others I'm here by accident, I don't belong here, it's a tragic mistake, but no-one believes me when I say so. They say: if you were born here, you belong here. Nor do I have any particular madness to contribute to this madhouse, though gazing at the scenery around me I can understand how it might be interpreted as holy, with its yellow nimbus rising and falling daily in the sky, and how my understanding might be construed as madness. Like the others I have a modest talent for hindsight and a knack for prophecy, but this does not certify me as mad. The madness produced for and by this house is a perfect kind of madness. It cannot be improved upon by, for example, an increase in the number of madmen, as the 'Safety in Numbers' theory advocated by our head psychiatrist would suggest. Our madhouse is small, replete with its own home-grown, genetically coded strain of madness, a guaranteed variety permeating every aspect of life. We are not simply mad men, women and children, but mad flora and fauna, mad stone and wind, mad history, mad quantum physics, mad archaeology, mad clinical psychology, even our madmen are mad and God himself is not immune from this kind of madness. It is a perfect madness, ours.

It needs neither more nor less mad things than are already con-tained in it. It can function, for instance, without recourse to that secret language developed during my incarceration here (namely now), a language unacknowledged by yet surviving within the interstices of the official language of madness. (If, for example, I thought this sentence through to its full articulation, the nurse would have to believe that I'm sipping a cup of coffee and smok-ing a cigarette.) But as I sip my coffee and smoke a cigarette the official language of madness thrives within its padded silence as a truly mad caper, a fiction we like to frolic in. A similar process occurs when a mad person dies. The mad gather round the corpse, reciting phrases to God, whom they have never seen yet trust unequivocally. Chanting words of faith, they watch the departed soul tracing its shadow in the snow, becoming ever fainter as it rises to heaven or descends to hell, as the case may be. Not one among these mad folk stops to look at the cold white miracle of snow. Not one points out that we are not living in the Alpine mountains but are irretrievably lost in the desert. And worst of all, no-one calls out: *Look, snow!* Instead a sociologist and a resi-dent anthropologist explain the phenomenon of purity, demon-strating through ancient rites how its enthronement serves to keep the mad mad, hence happy. And in the meantime something else has happened which has gone unnoticed: the opera's finale is missing, perhaps dissipated in holy air, or dissolved in the chaotic tears of the mad, who weep quietly to themselves till their dreams come true.

It is no tragedy that we cannot swallow soapsuds, but only their liquid residue. In fact for those of us intent on living it is a fortunate accident of nature, since soapsuds, devoid of any nutrients, may actually be harmful if swallowed in any substantial quantity. Some of us sometimes get the urge to cleanse the inside of our bodies, which is what prompted my little observation, but under no condition would I recommend soapsuds for the purpose, even if it were possible to swallow them. The madhouse went down to the beach today – madmen, madwomen, madchildren – not to bathe, though the weather was perfect for bathing, but to welcome outcasts of every description from lands overseas. Everyone assembled on the beach, supervised by Matron. We faced the open sea and let the surf wash our feet, and this too prompted my little observation on soapsuds and a clean body. Joyfully we bounced up and down on the sand as if to hurry the arrival of the outcasts from the other side of the sea. Then, in a succession of small waves, the dispossessed, degenerates, criminals, widows, orphans, families with all kinds of strange pets, and all sorts of hangers-on began to arrive as if out of nowhere, bringing with them whatever they could carry from beyond the horizon. At first only a dozen or so arrived at a time, but as the day progressed their numbers increased, and we welcomed them with open arms by the hundreds and thousands. The madhouse welcoming committee leapt up and down for joy to see how these folk, who had once put on great airs of normality, had abandoned old pretences and ambitions just to enter the fold of the madhouse. The madmen and madwomen became fruitful and begat (that very day) madchildren and madgrandchildren, thereby giving increase to our population and strengthening the foundations of our house for generations to come. That all this happened within the space of a single day, under perfect weather conditions and on a tiny stretch of beach, was nothing short of a miracle and was thus officially decreed by the authorities. Perhaps I remember the event with greater fondness than my fellow madmen because I am now in the enviable position of reclining inside my monthly bath, where I am free to think about God and the mysterious ways in which warm water cools and soapsuds slowly vanish. Matron walks in to check (to peep, I suspect) on my well-being. But as I'm completely covered with billowy clouds of suds, from my chin to my bloated big toes, only this meditative bobbing head above the surface is susceptible to her scrutiny. If she ever had the chance to act out her fantasies (which I can see, for thinking about God gives me that kind of vision) – not in this world but in another, where soapsuds may be the white fleshy part of an exotic fruit – she would swallow us all up alive, down to the bitter stone.

I reflect, said Robert, upon nothing which is exceptional or extraordinary in any way. I gaze at the mundane. It is nothing which any of us could not see or hear if we looked around us briefly once a day or even once in a lifetime. He was speaking in his usual way to a blank piece of paper that lay before him, awaiting a reply in the form of scribbly ink. Others called it writing, but Robert called it reflection. The glossy ink on the paper reflected his image dumbly, without understanding. The image was a cipher of Robert's attributes, his angles, rhythms, movements, physical or spiritual tics, and other facets of his being that somehow got compressed into the ink. Robert did not know how this process worked but it happened every day without fail. Once the ink dried up and lost its gloss, it tended to lie fallow in the grain of the paper, and during the course of a day's reflection all its attendant images evaporated in a matte of blackness. Robert did not mind being innocently misled by the ink in this way; it was a way of passing the time. Each of its marks was a casual step in a daily stroll, and the ink was a mirror continually shattered, fragmenting its own reflections like a puddle warped by a leaf, a footstep, or a light breeze. Exasperated by the burlesque appearance of his reflections, he sometimes dreamed of drawing the ink into his veins, absorbing it into the current of his blood so as to take nourishment from it and give it a semblance of life. Though he knew this was biologically impossible, the fantasy persisted all the same, and so, pen poised over paper, he formulated the problem as he spoke. Absurd – or interesting – he said to himself as he waited – to write as I do today, to describe what is self-evident whilst recalling what lies beyond the range of memory, namely in the immediate future, which is not prophecy, since time does not intervene between my description and its act. Robert found a correlation between his obsession to say anything, the marking of time with signs, and his obsession with failure. They seem to go hand in glove, he said. To fail and to write, to speak and to fall – these are not objects and their shadows but asymmetrical halves of an insoluble equation, free of all causality. Each moment of failure was a drop in the continuum of ink, and with each act of saying he foundered in its flux and was left stranded in its quickness. But what puzzled Robert about the task of writing was how the ink turned its inkness away from itself, how it faced him and formed a dark, detached and pristine image of his being, albeit two dimensional, yet clearly his own image, not another's, not some lofty authorial image he might have stumbled upon in the street. Despite his inherent scepticism about miracles, this seemed like a miracle nonetheless. But if it was an act of God (that is, a bona fide miracle) why should it be so well-suited to failure, to suffering and death, to every sort of affliction culminating in silence? Wouldn't we rather lie in the depths of the cosmos, he asked himself, within the quiet and modest affirmation of a sign, free inside the confines of its space, to see it, understand it and perhaps sanction it with the flurry of a signature? Regarding these questions Robert remained in the dark, scribbling over his scribbles to a solid black, mumbling prayers into the silence.

I am not myself. Uncertainty wraps me up in its amorphous arms and strangles me between the first person pronoun and my name. I say I, but mean Robert; say Robert, but mean I. If at times Robert means Robert, it is not always Robert Walser, the writer. There is a Robert Walser, writer, deceased. Nor have I ever been to, and do not recall, Switzerland. I have, however, collaborated with Robert in a primitive ritual that aimed to revive the landscapes of Heidi. We fail, we write. But my eyesight fails me, and my vision of time and place and person blurs into the wash of fiction. My optician tells me I would never qualify as a train driver or a pilot, so my childhood ambitions can be laid to rest. The problem, he says, is to delineate every crag and steeple disguised by a diaphanous fog settling over mountains and lakes. The fog skims over isolated cows and a chorus of neurotics scattered in the valley. The chorus is not an amateur theatre group, yet its members rehearse magical incantations with the precision of a circus troupe and with melodramatic nuances worthy of silent screen actors. The choristers are distant from, but within view of, each other. The idea of fog accompanied by cowbells in a meadow was implanted in my mind by Heidi on her visit to the Holy Land, before my first bout of depression; perhaps it caused it. Certain that it was his first and only depressive bout, Robert cannot remember being undepressed, not even during happy childhood hours. Diagnosed as schizophrenic, he accepts all medical opinion stoically and leaves its refutation to others. For my part, I wanted to kick up a fuss – but not Robert. He has gained a reputation as being officially mad, whilst unofficially remaining a nice, gentle, kind-hearted soul. The Swiss take umbrage at being called mad. To be diagnosed as schizophrenic, my optician tells me, is in itself cause for depression, whilst being depressed is not necessarily a schizophrenic condition. Unless, he says, your depression happens on alternate days or at regular intervals. Depending on your etymological bias, he says, your schizophrenia may be based on a split mind, a torn heart, or a ruptured diaphragm. If a singer stops singing, it may well be due to her schizophrenia; on the other hand, a forlorn lover may attempt to lavish his affections on anti-depressant tablets, the chemical grail of comfort. When Moses shattered the tablets of the Law, God turned schizoid. The incident, you will recall, was provoked by a metallic cow. I was dreaming of God's meadow as Heidi entered the Holy Land with the music of cowbells. I was reminded of a crucifixion and a resurrection, and an ascension with a forty-day time lapse. Psychic though it was, I could not fathom the logic in that chain of events. After resurrection on such a grand scale, Heaven must have been anti-climactic. But Heidi reassured me: In future the mystery behind the event will be revealed in the Second Coming, with live-action replay of our sins. I took her word for it and kept quiet, comparing her golden hair to the sun. At night I slipped in under the covers, curled up beside her and watched her sleep. What I saw was like the eye of God, I imagined, before he let light be. Her hair fell to her shoulders, from where it was only a hand's breadth to her breasts. Piously I bowed my head into her body, imagining a bowl of milk, and leaned forth to nourish my infant self, reclaiming the fable of milk and honey in the passion of semen and ovum.

Robert stood under *The Waterfall*, veiled in its spray as if he had just written it. Whether his or not, it cleansed him. Uttering the word 'go' from the depths of his throat, he stood paralysed like a corpse before re-awaking and offered an innocuous greeting to death as it passed him. Then he fell. It was a point of quiescence, fixed in our imagination like a smile. A wad of ink-covered papers lay rotting under the snow. Seeking to command movement and direction, he fell backwards into the snow, slowly, onto a patch of icy flakes. A collapse into childhood, he thought, a flight from one memory to another in pursuit of the freedom promised by death. Now we are both there, lost like nervous mites in a whirlwind. Retracting poems from obscurity, one poet burns them in a searing light, another seals them in a dead language. Robert thought no end would come to his fall, no gravity would survive its own force. Before him stretched a blank sheet of paper, impregnable, unable to absorb the least drop of ink into its frozen gape. He stepped forward, then back, then ceased, as if expecting a music – a choir of angels perhaps – that would let him regain his bearings. He was about to exchange words with spirits from another world, but the madness business in his head distracted him, a sickness and nuisance which he squeezed out of existence like a pimple, letting a word erupt from his parted lips: 'go', he breathed. I am writing about Robert of my own volition, bearing responsibility without shame or resentment. Despite the curtain of darkness that fell over us, his brush with divinity implicated me, made me the angel of neutral benevolence by his side. My mind was crammed with essential delusions. I prepared to make a speech in his honour. I wanted to bury him, leave nothing in his wake, and conclude his life with a durable stone. At such times our dealings with death often lapse into vague theological promises, picture-book images that would shame a child. When the word exploded I saw a direction that did not exist before, and took it. Robert remained passive. Underneath the wetness of the snow he felt the wetness of the forthcoming grasses and of rains a thousand years hence. His body oozed out its pale fluids onto a clump of damp earth, inscribing a little remark, a final pert observation: 'gone'. From there contradictions developed – they did not simply erupt like cyclamens on stony Mediterranean hillsides – into harmonics, out of which Robert's perennial pains issued.

Robert crossed the street and ate a sandwich. Reflexively, without intent, he hailed a cab, and the cab, correctly misreading his signal, failed to stop. He sat down at a bus stop and remembered how he had once urinated in an alley, how a dog had come along, how he had patted it on the head and thought of Diogenes and his dog-friends. He recalled how he combed his hair that morning before setting out on his errands. Robert crossed with the light, not against it, treading with a sense of civic pride. He sat down at the bus stop to rest, not to wait, then got up again to cross back to the other side. He was not colour-blind, nor removed from humanity, so when the light changed he crossed with the crowd and felt the warmer for it. As he crossed the street he talked to a nurse. He told her how he had once hammered a coin flat, then flatter, how he once tasted mouldy cheese as if he'd been starving, in desperation. Robert then browsed in a bookshop and a few days later, recollecting the book-lined shelves, repeated his action on a privet growing by the pavement. Now he spoke softly to himself, using words that nobody understood or heard properly, and received sidelong glances from passers-by, quick sharp darts, sometimes longer gazes. He crossed the street one more time, then again for the sake of symmetry. During intervals between crossings he performed other actions. That day Robert crossed the street several times. He rubbed his eyes like a cartoon character he knew intimately and recalled other actions which he'd performed long ago or recently, or actions he had planned to carry out in future. It made no difference to him when exactly such actions were performed, because sooner or later, he thought, past and future would coalesce. Every memory of an action was an informed repetition, so any memory of any action would suit him. When he had no memory of any particular action he would invent a new one, subjecting it to rigorous memory tests. He crossed the street more often than he remembered crossing the street, and when he noticed this curious little anomaly he set about amending his actions, so that he would always have more actions than memories of actions to call upon. But as he had no proof of such actions, his memories became somewhat doubtful and he often needed to think for a while before exposing them to the light of day or, when necessary, hiding them out of sight. Robert lay in the snow in the white Alpine mountains, his lips pressed lightly against a small mound of accumulated flakes. He seemed to kiss the snow, and as he kissed it, the kiss seemed a whisper. His breath left a momentary trace of his passion in its dissolution, and he saw its image dissolve in the future. Then he crossed the street for its own sake, a pure and unsymbolic trek against the light. His steps seemed measured to the end of time as he crossed the street and kissed the snow in one and the same breath.

Contradictions raged in Robert's head as he awoke, depressed, surprised by his own awakening. Ignore what needs to be ignored, he counselled himself, and let the prose ramble within the limits of memory. Loss of desire, direction, appetite, a general atrophy that looked suicidal, a fear of success – these things kept him happy in the madhouse. He cultivated a subdued dialogue with the image of clarity, aiming to articulate it clearly until the image could manifest itself. Without being sophist about it, he could not illuminate the air through which he gasped. Its relentless transparency turned the madhouse into his morning star, so that at daybreak he sighed, full of wonder and despair over such constancy. Robert reminded his audience that he had forgotten what the stories were doing in his writing, that they were intended to be forgotten at some point before or after writing. Blown off course by gusts of music, chimes of falling snow, he could not say what came when or who belonged where. Death affected his language, wavering between extremes of memory and empty spaces of oblivion, as the smallest words revealed the biggest ambitions. His desire to expose the hidden face of clarity gave death a certainty, though certainty itself, like the outline of angels' wings through fog, was merely an echo of clarity obscured by music. Yet his death washed over these differences. Opinions round him grew flaccid and dubious, and his audience perished or survived according to the daily dosage of their medication. Things remained unresolved. Being anti-sophist would not have resolved anything.

Here our madhouse exists in the fulfilment of its description: loose phrases, disjointed syllables, hollow paragraphs and torrents of words cover the walls. Cushioned between bedtime and dawn, we lie wrapped in fantasies extracted from language. Tourists refuse to read our dreams yet pay for the privilege of a visit at a rate linked to the setting sun's velocity. Blinded by events around them, they escape from home and inadvertently learn the new language. When they visit the madhouse death pokes everywhere, yet they do not know the words for 'here' or 'there', and if it stares them in the face they gape back mutely like plastic statues. In summer, distinguished from other tourists by their specialised interests, they visit the war in the east. Simulating a battlefield, all the prams in the madhouse move at the same speed, face the same direction, bear the same identity markings, advance, retreat or hold their position in uniform formations. Cries from the prams are historical verses in code, we learn, renditions of rubber-stamped orders divinely ordained and sealed behind numbered doors in hallowed government corridors. Like visions, the orders come from above. In the madhouse gravity quashes those orders in the glare of mirrors. Robert awoke, dismayed that gravity prevented him from flying. As he looked up at the sky a flat suspension of faith hovered above him. Without a word he took his next step towards clarity and entered the line of fire through the imaginary open window.

He lifted his head from the tabletop and levelled his eyeline. I realised at that point that I may have lied. Robert arrived here some twenty or thirty years ago. Now he has just raised his head to acknowledge the place. He says it feels so familiar. This is a form of happiness, we confess blindly to each other. We are not in the snow, not in the sand, yet the landscape around us is given to extremes. I'm not here to write, he informs his enquirer, but to be mad. Once again we are on the inside edge of a madhouse. Its function is not to be mad but to contain the mad, as though in a soft skin. Outside the madhouse the possibility of madness has been reduced to a prevalent itch. Robert saw how grammar delights in the presentation of things (for example, the table on which his head has been drooping half a lifetime) and how things placed upon or moving around them (ants scavenging for breadcrumbs, bees sucking on sugar grains) delight in their own representation. He saw in these things – tables, insects, people who called on him from time to time to say hello or goodbye – the incarnation of writers most likely to be himself. There was a premise to his madness, which he liked to illustrate: I strike a match and set the house ablaze, but the house extinguishes itself immediately. You see, the match falls into the snow, the match is the house, of course, and the snow lies on the ground, descended from a dark and brooding sky. You see, he says. Then he adjusts his tie. The passion is the flickering afterglow of a thought, that is all. Robert tries hard to be mad, acting as if he were not here to write. When I lie to him about the conflagration of the world he wants to hear more, wants to visualise the fire and understand the physics of its heat. I'm waiting for him to topple backwards into the snow, for his hat to roll down the slope, for flies to emerge out of frozen larvae and settle nervously but quietly upon his dead eyes. The gravity of our madhouse has enclosed the frontiers of grammar, so that after the fall he continues to fall, without a wink. He does not blink or smile either, being dead, though his body still seems paralysed by extreme shyness.

I was given the task of writing the description of what happened. I said that Robert fell backwards, not into snow but into crystallised drops of childhood. As he fell he heard his mother's voice, or its essence, intensified by the act of dying, a sound like the voice he called his mother's. He responded with a prolonged sigh which illustrated his idea that happiness is a false coin, too easily desired, more easily forfeited. Without developing into a smile, a grin was slapped across his face, masking a cold, hopeless lamentation. Almost dead or perhaps already dead, he received permission to move to an adjacent field of memory (like a butterfly, symbolising a soul, flitting from world to world) but declined it. His mind would not collude with death, so he continued to fall, as described above. During and after gravity he found only more gravity, nothing else. I write these things with a sense of guilt, a sense in which Robert is almost or perhaps already dead, depending on style, the frequency of adjectives, or spelling errors. There is no other sense, just the one, as is evident from the snow which is white and the corpse lying discoloured against it. Nor is there common sense between us, only love. Having drunk the condensation of my breath, I look into the mirror, adjusting the syntax, squinting into the grammar, while the scene transpires into an erasure: snow falling on fresh snow, the slow elimination of a corpse. If there were a face in the mirror, it would not smile. Even if a hint of a smile appeared by chance, it would be false, hewn out of abstraction, posing a question incapable of bearing my response. Such inquisitions are the norm in our mad-house, where we keep a log of events. I was only given the job of writing it all down, word by word, for Matron — *Nothing too fancy, understand? Just shades of white!* — she who has been out to lunch all day, hounding our self-expression.

He would have preferred not to collapse into madness but to enter majestically in broad daylight, head held high, gazing into a burning sun. He would have preferred not to slip secretly under cover of dusk in a snowy landscape, yet he slipped all the same. It was always dusk, always snowy. Although not there to write, as he claimed, Robert wrote *The Waterfall* in the madhouse. His thoughts raced ahead of his own disclaimers, drops of water cascading headlong through his brain, inundating his eyes. The difficulty was not to abstain from writing but to know where and how to fall (backwards into the snow), how to cease to fall, if necessary – if, say, a nymph emerged from the spray to embrace him – and how to grace his fall with a dignified step. Robert soon learned how to be identified as mad and how to certify his new identity. He learned how to chain himself to the discomfiting fixtures of madness in a professional and business-like manner. But he fell. For a moment he suffered the shame of having once contemplated a writing of a different, older, more familial and familiar order of words. He wrote a sentence in an elegiac mood, without fretting over its style, and when he saw himself as its subject it pleased him. So much so that he wrote it again in a new hand. The sentence emerged out of his own body and he regarded it as his legitimate offspring. It also pleased him to have an audience that recognised him as the figure of *The Walker* or the body in *The Waterfall.* The sentence passed. It fell downward like rain, then seeped away, and like rain it suddenly stopped. Robert lay on the rocks, at the edge of an eddy, exhilarated by his body's stillness as measured against the chaos of churning water all around him. It pleased him to be on the brink of death, inside his head, from where he could look on idly and without comment. Being dead or on the verge of death, he was unable to pass comment on what he saw, unable to judge distance, that much was understood. I too saw the glaze on his face in that way, not just as water glistening on a dead man's face. I abandoned the body quickly and quietly, cleanly and openly, as if at sea. Perhaps for that reason I'm sometimes unnaturally drawn to the sea, sometimes breaking off in mid-sentence to look upon the sea as someone I know, someone uttering sentences out of the blue, uttering words I may have said myself.

I have left a few blank pages in my last scribblings book, wrote Robert, in order not to delay the scribblings in the new book. He sat and mused over the words he had written as well as those he had not yet written, words withheld from general view or held in abeyance till their meanings caught up with them. He mused, waiting for his muse to act, now, before it was too late. What action did Robert want the muse to perform? He thought that was up to the muse to decide – he had had enough to cope with as it was. I'd like to inscribe its crisp virgin leaves, to possess this new book, he wrote. A fog settled round him everywhere, engulfing both muse and scribblings. I do not understand this lust for the voluptuous and voluminous, he confessed, but it is already mine, and I notice how strange that halfway through its first page, having scribbled a few words, I have nothing more to say. So he sat and mused. They were words, therefore common property, irrespective of their private or public meanings, and so, he said, insubstantial and lethal. Lethal? How? Robert asked the page. They were lethal, self-evidently so, he said. Oh, Mallarmé! he sighed, singing. How we might collaborate! Stupidly this century calls you back and stupidly I'm blind to your return. I kiss your hand, again. My name is Robert Walser and I, too, like Robert Walser, am not so mad after all, but only as mad as you. Robert thought the word he had lost in this paroxysm of emotion, or perhaps the word he had hoped to invent out of it, or the word on the tip of his tongue, or on the tip of another's tongue, was *meditation.* But it seems he was hearing things, for as he prepared to substantiate this hunch, a familiar voice stepped into the room, softly at first, then in a lacerating pitch full of sinister nuances in its tone, and announced the time for medication. Robert reached through the fog for the infertile words he had scribbled as preparatory notes for a suicide note. He crumpled them up in his fist and tossed the absent paper on which they were pencilled into an imaginary fire, drawing unreal comfort from the warmth emanating out of nowhere. *And how are we today, monsieur Mallarmé?* said the voice, vanishing back into the air.

The madness business in Robert's head was going to be treated by a psychiater in therapy sessions on Thursdays and other days at eleven o'clock – that is, he and the psychiater would discuss and analyse his head. Robert thought that eleven o'clock was a bad time to delve into the madness business, since at that time of day on Thursdays, as on every other day, his head was too busy inventing sentences which he wrote out in longhand on sheets of paper lying flat under that very head. The sentences came from a less chaotic region in his head, and he felt that to delve into the madness business right in the middle of the sentence business was to court confusion and disaster. But Robert was a courteous man, so when the psychiater said there was really no choice but to deal with the madness business at that time, he politely acquiesced – *All right, eleven o'clock, then* – and braced himself for the inevitable disaster. When Thursday came he stopped in mid-sentence, put on a fireman's helmet, a pair of rubber boots and a fireman's coat, then picked up his fireman's axe and set off down the corridor to confront the problem which the madness business (or rather the psychiater's insistence on its treatment) had precipitated. The result was predictable. The madhouse headlines screamed: HACK HACKS QUACK! But what happened was really more metaphorical, albeit executed in the style of living theatre (as if a small metaphor had escaped that day into the wider metaphorical world). Robert returned to his room and, at the request of the coroner, filled out an official report regarding his session. He employed sentences which he had just invented on his way back from the psychiater, sentences charged with emotion and with highly graphic descriptions of the session. He infused his sentences with a sense of hope which, though it lent the report a certain grace, unfortunately blunted the magic of their invention. The coroner made a considerable effort to understand his sentences, but he could only do so by reading them out loud and interpreting each one literally. So whilst Robert anticipated the coroner's appreciation of his literary efforts, he was in fact immediately sent to see the madhouse executive committee, who in turn arranged for a psychiater to deal with the madness business in his head. Once again Robert made himself comfortable in an armchair as the psychiater asked: "Will Thursdays at eleven o'clock be all right?" "Of course," said Robert with a gesture of fatigue and resignation, then momentarily let his mind drift behind closed eyelids. As we sometimes dream and think simultaneously just before falling off to sleep, so Robert spirited himself into an upright chair from which he was unable to break free: his limbs and torso were strapped into the seat by thick leather thongs, coloured wires criss-crossed his body, electrodes were hooked up to a metal cap on his head, his wrists and ankles were secured with iron clasps, and his lips were glued tightly together. Breathing through his nostrils, he could barely discern a calm voice in the room: *Are we comfortable?* Between the voice and the black sleep that followed there were all kinds of things now vague and forgotten. Robert wondered if the voice was speaking to him or if it was part of a dialogue coming from another world, an exchange of words he may have imagined that day, weighted with a judgement on his life.

Titles baffled him anyway. Recall, said Robert to himself, words and numbers falling through the mind's waterfall just before it evaporates into a thin obscure air. Isolate the force in a large glass structure supported by a concrete framework and see it flow silently in a steady surge, quietly like an involuted fountain. Site it in a desert landscape where a few desolate plants grow among scattered rocks and a group of children plays in the background. The air is parched, the sun oppressive. An hour of psychotherapy has its own continuum, he recalled, materialising out of nowhere like clouds in an empty sky, then condensing or evaporating with cool nonchalance. The therapist, they told him, is not exactly a psychiater but more of a doctor and a friend rolled into one – his name sits on the horizon of memory and his speech is in retreat behind it. Robert was intrigued by the mystery of healing, wondering how in hell it worked. One moment I was speaking to myself, the next, he recalled, he appeared out of nowhere like a cloud in a desert, as sometimes happens in dreams, saying: "What do *you* think?" The relationship in our language, he said, is a suspension of coital pauses, intense pregnant silences whose risk of miscarriage is proportionate to the number of words not yet uttered. We can neither extricate ourselves from this absurd pose nor arrive at any conclusive decisions about its meaning or shape. All the while we are being observed by the eyes of Robert Walser,

half-buried in snow, sinking into that whiteness where death re-
curs like a childhood dream. The words of our coitus function
intermittently, with a resounding thrill whenever meanings either crystallise or fragment. But the gravity of this comedy is
random, someone said in the room. We prepare the heart, the
lungs and other organs (mine as well as yours) for a future trans-
plant. We hoard each other's reserves and our words flow through
each other's veins, leaping from one body to the other without a
second thought. The joke is on me, thought Robert, and it's
weighted like a lead balloon. Our roomful of speech is one of
those fatal accidents – there are so many, the statistics are stagger-
ing – so that another body, a stranger to our intercourse, must be
mutilated if either of us is to reap any benefit from this consum-
mate laughter. He believed that acid rain and radioactive fallout
(like natural disasters) had been replaced by a fancy theology whose
deity incarnated a dream in the future tense, a Messianic visionary without the bread of peace in his hand. My own preference
for catastrophe has always favoured the dead forest at noon, its
wan and irremediable gloom blanketing my head, warding my
thoughts from the rays of the sun.

On bad days Robert found his sentences repugnant and offensive, provocations against thought. The madness business in his head had relinquished grammar and poetics long ago. Regardless of its invention, charm or style, literary artifice revolted him, and he felt a particular loathing for that incestuous circle of scribblers – in fact, anti-scribblers masquerading as scribblers – who promoted each other's texts. Like master carpenters, they were good at making solid coffins for each other, their texts composed of old pieces of wood planed and polished according to their moral prepossessions. As for his own sentences, it was not their intent that disturbed him but the aura of sublimation behind it, oozing out vaporous swampy substances upon the calm beatitude of chartered words. Despicable and shameful, thought Robert (and I agreed – he was beginning to rave), to scribble such sentences as if to make a poem, the confluence of thoughts disgorged in afterthoughts, the product of a labouring mind in a field of delusions where only illusions survived. Besides, he thought, how could these things be made if their maker, devising sets of meanings to quantify sounds, were not making it up, that is, faking it, during the process of making? On such days his ego was flaccid, halfdead, a bloated and putrid body, a bad-smelling thing swelling out of the ground. Would it not be better (he thought) to be a body drowned with waterlogged lungs and a stark silence blistering on its purple tongue? Standing grave and upright, without understanding, he continued to have these thoughts. The image

of his execution, it occurred to him, was not a picture but a hurt-
ful odour lingering in the air, a torture reluctantly suffered in
pleasure, its pain felt only when his mind gave the sign of pain-
fulness. You cannot imagine, he said, and it was precisely so. You
must retorture the tortured, he added. Flayed alive, a picture survived (in a book, no less) and what was destroyed could not and
(by definition) did not. A skinless person screaming in agony
through a silent picture, his conscience adopting the role of a
forsaken lover hurriedly opening a letter, in consequence of which
he is doomed. In those situations Robert did not want to die
especially. Even while trudging knee-deep through oblivion, he
wanted to remember. During interludes, as memory gave way to
some malodorous muse, death split the torso open, exposing the
raw burning hole that gaped wide open for Robert's comfort and
eternal rest. For the most part, however, his relationship with
death was verbal – but for that one virginal submission of heads
– and he lived out the rest of his life in obscurity, with the com-
pendium of torture and depravity by his bedside.

The object on the table lying on its back in front of me is my recent right hand. In a sense it is still mine, but physically we're no longer connected. We've been separated by the brutal chop of a butcher's cleaver wielded by my left hand out of frustration with the right hand's posturing phrases. Though I used to use it for other purposes besides writing, it was during a particularly clumsy sentence that my left hand took it upon itself to act as judge and executioner in dealing with the right hand's crime. I say "crime" but this is perhaps an exaggerated verdict for the act of writing, however incompetent. Now it lies perfectly motionless. I do sense some feelings in it, however, feelings that would normally be associated with fingers wriggling or rolling a cigarette or maybe scribbling. When I touch my severed hand with my left hand I become trapped in an overwhelming sadness. So I try to refrain from doing so. Instead I stare at it, transfixed by its solitude, riveted like an eye dazzled by the sun. But there's no movement, unless I give it a little nudge, a push, shoving it slightly like a rocking horse. With the exhilaration of such a hopeless movement comes the desperate remoteness in its touch. My arm – in fact, my whole body apart from its lost appendage – feels different. This is natural, I suppose. I'm referring not simply to the physical pain or the emotional longing to be re-integrated with my hand – this has been forfeited for good, I know – but to that stark indifference I encountered when I saw you in the mirror, that sense of being cast off, de-centered and left to muse on

the absence of your body as an object neglected and reflected —
though reflected in what, I wonder. The feeling has never left me.
I need only shut my eyes for a split second if I wish to re-experi-
ence the mystery evoked by your body's reflection, without a trace
of its physical presence around me. It was not a trick of the light,
not a play of the mind, just as this dead hand lying in front of me
is no hallucination. Only the pool of blood gives the scene a sense
of indulgence, a scent of gore. Sooner or later these things are
erased, even now as I bite through my lower lip to alleviate the
pain wracking my body. But let's talk about that later, at a more
convenient time, said Robert, when the pain has finally subsided.
I touched it once again to see if it would come alive. I thought its
fingers might offer a little gesture, a little miracle, like waving
good-bye.

A film is being made by Robert Walser, dead, lying in the snow on location. On the face of it the activity of a corpse presents a problem. But it is undoubtedly his corpse. Walser is not dying, is not on his deathbed, but decidedly dead. Yet we have to concede that he is making this film. There is nothing figurative or symbolic about it. By reputation I'm like a dog, a *cynic*, and go around with dogs. Though the epithet is based on rumour, I'm proud to say that it was I who instigated it, because there's a lot of truth in it, virtually the whole truth. I love dogs, strays in particular, though I speak for only one, myself. When howling or barking I prefer to use "we", as aristocratic nuances trip that much more easily off my tongue. We talked our way into the film and came out talking, as if we'd spent the film's duration fast asleep, mumbling, as indeed we had. Being very dead while making a film is not as fantastic as it might seem, and while the corpse of Robert Walser directs the scene our ideologies remain intact. We know what we like, even more in the dark. The afternoon sky is grey, the air crisp. Emerging from the snow, like Lazarus in a clown's costume, Robert Walser rises to the occasion – his brow, his bristly chin, his hair and overcoat imperfectly caked with white flakes – while I, Diogenes, wag my tail. Stiffly he picks up his hat from the snow. It's all very moving, very life-like, as if some god were directing from beyond the clouds. We're adapting George Büchner's story, *Lenz*. Our hero is a poet who is having a nervous

breakdown and is metaphorically lost in the mountains. His poetry is conveyed obliquely in Büchner's subtle prose. Robert renders that prose in turn poetic through the invisible music of his cinematic vision. (Lately Robert and I have grown closer and are on first name terms – he calls me Dog.) With that stiff gait and icy blood of his, that pinpoint gaze across the mountains, only Robert is capable of bringing to the screen, as we say, the profound complexities of Lenz. True, Lenz is a lunatic – but aren't we all? Robert, too, is unwell. When Alex the Great arrived the other day and asked what he could do for us, we said: Please move, you're blocking the light! The pack of us were in a barrel, basking in the sunshine and minding our own business, when the Emperor came seeking favours from dogs. Who but a total madman would behave like that? And when our producer, Schreber, enquired how the film was coming along, Robert said: *I'm not here to make pictures, I'm here to be mad!* Now we appreciate the subtle distinctions between scenery and sanity. We have regulations to abide by and behavioural patterns to imitate and perfect. But it is still in our interest to show some personality quirk – the hook, as we say – when seeking entry to this snow-capped part of the country. When they asked me my name I growled, so they called me the Dog.
Thus, gnawing a bone, Diogenes paused.

We were saying, we are in the mountains making a film under the direction of Robert Walser, deceased. We wag our tail because he has at last risen and made his way to the next scene. By coincidence the hero and the actor playing the hero's part share the name of Lenz. They say that Robert auditioned and hired him over the phone on the basis of that name. He had looked it up in the phone directory, which lists several in our region, and offered the part to the first Lenz who had heard of his literary namesake and would be available to start work immediately. Of the other Lenz's, one was constantly engaged, one had had his phone disconnected, two never answered (later we learned they were brothers who wintered in the south), while the majority put down the phone thinking that Robert was selling equity shares in a film production. In fact our own Lenz (a film buff who habitually entered competitions) at first thought he had won a prize and therefore agreed to everything before he realised what was happening. Now he seems happy enough in his role, though "happy" may be a slight misnomer. Let's say he has not yet saddened. In fact when he was asked to play the part, he was so impressed, so flattered (though he knows nothing about Lenz apart from a street with that name in his home town), that his witless face still beams radiantly during rehearsals, despite the director's recent death and resurrection. We begin to wonder if

he may not be just a bit too gormless, perhaps an idiot. With Robert dead in the snow, or rising out of the snow, it is impossible to change the cast, and the prospect of having Büchner's melancholic hero played in the film with a perpetual grin on his face is a depressing one. And it's ironic that our Mr Lenz refuses to show any signs of depression in his real-life face and yet has the extraordinary capacity to memorise perfectly those distinctly uncheerful lines. Glumly we tuck our tail between our legs. Little could he have suspected that Robert Walser would drop dead in the snow on the first day of principal photography or that the film would be made by his corpse. We wonder if Mr Lenz is some sort of opportunist waiting to take advantage of the situation. Maybe there's a Hollywood agent beckoning from the valley below. We snarl, baring our teeth in the long shadows. And yet he seems to have adjusted himself to all these anomalies, as most of us have, and as the first day of principal photography draws to a close, it is becoming clear that the real Lenz, like Robert Walser himself, will somehow fail to turn up. Even now, as he recites those depressing lines (brilliantly, despite that stupid grin), his eyes roll heavenward in a way which has become symptomatic of this film, as if he were seized by visions or an apprehension of poetic justice swooping down on all of us.
Then Diogenes lay low, ears cocked, and fell silent.

It had to be explained to him that the fundamental rule did not…demand the thinking out of an idea, but certainly the complete utterance of what had been thought. He required many admonitions, however, before he learnt this.

—Sandor Ferenczi

He surrendered his private punctuation for the sake of the other's form of sentencing, a form incapable of discerning a pause or the blink of an eye. He lay on his back facing away from the other, gazing at the ceiling or the wall, or studying the picture fixed to the wall like a trophy. He would enter the cinema late, he confessed, his dog tightly reined in by the collar. The therapist refers everything to the self, while the self in turn diverts it to an ongoing movie. So these pieces evoke lost images from a film projected in your mind. You enter as the house lights dim and struggle to find a seat in the violet darkness, half-heartedly trying to make out what goes on on the screen whilst focusing your attention on the search for the best available seat. You settle for a perspective that seems wrong, having failed to find your proper seat. Let's say you have no real place in the world and the film's opening images remain unassimilated in your perception of things. You wonder how crucial these first images really are. Whatever its artistic value, the film signals your embarkation on a private tragedy. All of this is spoken by the therapist with a deliberate tone of voice. One of us is enjoying himself. The semi-darkness of the cinema is unreal, a sickly, tainted half-light reflecting off the screen, jumping convulsively with every image it projects, images you've missed as much as those that will soon consume you. We've grown accustomed to such little disasters in our time, the self responds. Our pieces are born already lost in the semi-obscurity of their creation. And if sometimes the screening occurs outdoors, the illusion of darkness is manufactured by the stratagem of folding chairs lined up in rows in the open air at dusk, with a sea breeze playing at the hem of reality. We bundle them all together, these little dances, under the blushing rubric of Robert Walser, model of selfhood breathing his last in the mountain air. The recurrent rhythm is that of a waltz, the therapist notes, and the dialogue is in 3/4 time. So the pieces are not Swiss-German in tone, not Walserian in character after all, we discover together, and I suppose you could never really dance to them. Oh!? There are times I'd like to reach the end of our little speculations, he says, relax in a foreign country (be close to home, near the womb) and leave the self to the other. At other times, however, I explore the madness business all around us, which leaves me no time to travel.

Are we still waltzing? One-two-three… One-two-three… The heart of our music is a ground bass of gyration, a necessity of turning which I, as therapist, must emphasise in order to establish the circuit of our dance. But I can't rely on your indirect speech, which too frequently falters and leaves me puzzled as to your whereabouts. So I've taken the liberty of transposing your scribblings. They delineate a figure in the Holy Land, an emissary from the madness business stumbling upon the discovery that God *is the opposite of Rodin. Your ambiguous words chill to the bone and the scent of death permeates the air. Whatever is repeated now has never been uttered before. You had a thought and sat down. You had already been seated earlier, before getting up to stretch your legs. You walked around for a while before sitting down again and thought about your thought. These things had happened before and now happen again. Your re-telling is a leapfrogging to the conclusion of the phrase* "In the beginning…" *You did not put ink to paper as you used to do whenever a thought occurred to you. It was not that kind of thought. It would not translate into another form, written or drawn, nor into a simple action. It was a thought which you classified as pure — of, for, by itself. Abstract thought. Rather than applying the thought, which would have been impossible in any case, you sat down, as if beneath or beside it. You thought about how it could not be dealt with in any manner whatsoever and how, on the other hand, it could not simply be discarded or ignored, could not be dumped on the scrapheap of all your thoughts. The experience pleased and disturbed you. Incommunicable though it was, it seemed as if the thought had somehow fallen into place and made perfect sense of your life and everything to do with your life. You were both pleased and disturbed to be yourself, and this mani- fested your joy and your suffering. This is where we came in, having adjourned and resumed the dance. Our feet have grown stupid with fatigue, as the refrain recurred more often than we'd anticipated at the outset of this guesswork.*

Robert had no mission in life. He was not like Jesus Christ and had no trade to fall back on either. Despite his love of wood and a propensity to record his thoughts in writing, he was neither a carpenter nor a teacher of creative writing. He was not a busi- nessman, a drug dealer, a television presenter or anything like that. He was not involved in things which might have led di- rectly or indirectly to any measure of success. He was marked for failure as others are marked for success. He had worked, on and off, as a clerk, a gardener, a night watchman, a hospital orderly and in dozens of other menial jobs, more often *off* than *on*. As days and weeks passed with each successive job, the tedium of it would get the better of him and he would quit in order to devote more time to his little thoughts. Occasionally he held a job for a whole year. He was in the habit of recording his thoughts in ink, that is, of writing them down on scraps of paper or in little scribblings books which he carried with him everywhere. Later on he acquired a typewriter, still later a computer, but he rarely used these machines except for finalising his thoughts or for mak- ing fair copies, as he called it. But over the years he found it less and less desirable, indeed unnecessary, to make these final drafts, since such labour could never equal the pleasure he got from the flow of ink with the initial scribbling down of a thought – an experience he likened to bleeding, as though the ink oozing from the nib of his pen (a fountain pen, of course) had its origin in his veins. It goes without saying, Robert uttered quietly inside his head, that the marks I make to represent some thought are not imprints or traces of that thought but skewed and random symbols whose composite form is somehow understood as a definitive idea. So if I write a thought the words can only relate it obliquely and thereby manufacture a little black white lie – which is the way my editor reads these things (even though I have no editor, I still collaborate in this device). With respect to a career, then, Robert was universally regarded as a failure (yet by his own account he saw himself primarily as a thinker and only secondarily, once his life's experiences confirmed it, as a *bona fide* failure), and all his endeavours would invariably end in that distinctive lack of success which was to become his trademark. There were even times when his failure seemed a foregone conclusion, irrespective of any effort or lack of it he might have given to a particular job or to some independent project he had undertaken. This despite his persistent fantasies of climbing the ladder of success to the apex of some profession or other, fantasies often triggered by questions on application forms: *Why do you want to be a cleaner?* or *Who will be your readership?* As when, for example, applying for a gardener's job, he imagined his future as Director of Gardens at the Holy Land Municipality Office. As for those around him, they "saw it coming a mile off" (his failure, not the Directorship), though no-one had the courage, or perhaps the opportunity (if we allow them the benefit of doubt), to warn him of the dangers that lay in his path. To some extent Robert himself saw it coming, albeit with hindsight, and he harboured a secret pride in having coaxed his lack of success along from time to time and in becoming a kind of self-made failure. Not that he didn't suffer for his pains or that his obsession with failure was easy to sustain. Nights and days consumed him as he bemoaned his fate. Sleepless, tear-drenched nights were whiled away in futile cogitation on the impossibility of things in general, while the days were occupied with wrenching the same vague thoughts from his head, quenching them in a dumb annihilation as he wandered through dirty streets and shied away from friends and strangers alike. In short, he had a bad time of it, a time the doctor had described as "those disjunctive phases in your life" and which summed up his dysfunctional life. Even from Robert's own point of view, such disjunctive phases were mere twinkles in a much broader and deeper history, and it seemed that things which either happened or failed to happen to him were nothing but minor incidents buried in the remote past, lost in some corner of the world, so that he now resigned himself to the totality of failure, settling with an obliging equanimity into his newly acquired position in the world, and effectively found a kind of happiness within it. Of course he realised that no promotion or demotion existed at this level of reality, that every act had to be performed to perfection within its own perverse limitations, and that each thought must occur to him unequivocally, with a simple but grim determinacy. *Is there* (he wondered quietly in his head) *a kind of beauty in this mess?* Since things could not possibly get worse, they must be as best as they could ever get, must be at that stage of having reached their pinnacle, and so within that range of circumstances he could not conceive of any threat or promise fomenting beyond his own horizon nor see anything that might be construed as change, whether for better or worse. Unless, he whispered to himself in a muted panic, I fail at failure. He wondered if that were possible. He calculated what the odds were of that happening, what the possibility was for such a sadistic twist of fate in his life, and the thought crossed his mind at least once in that lifetime. Whilst he appreciated the irony of it, surely there were limits to its application even within his own liberal cast of mind. Not that such failure could lead to success, but rather something far worse, something so terrifyingly worse that he could not quite put his finger on it. He wondered long and hard if that sort of thing were possible in this advanced technological day and age of ours, if something so much worse than his failing at failure could come along, something insufferable, incommunicable, infinitely worse than the thought he had just had in his head, the thought he had glimpsed before sitting down, before rising again, before falling, just before dying in the snow. He began thinking other thoughts, thoughts about specific things, concrete thoughts about reality (as some called it), dialectical thoughts and thoughts on the nature of the universe, political, psychoanalytical and psycholinguistic thoughts, mathematical thoughts and thoughts about the weather, thoughts about his clothes and thoughts about timetables and thoughts about time itself. And in this maze of thoughts he suddenly remembered his own thought hinging on the word *failure,* as if it had leapt out of a dictionary and was staring him woundedly between the eyes, and he noted its Latin source, *fallere* to deceive, be concealed from, escape observation, be ignorant of, and how it may be related to Greek *phelos* deceitful, and to Sanskrit *hrunati* he gets lost, and to Old Slavic *zulu* bad, evil. And he imagined salvation proffered to him through the word's clumsy syllables, as if it were beckoning to him from the depths of his own consciousness like the sign of an ancient covenant, propped up by the superstition of etymology, whose priest chanted primitive blessings: I have not forsaken you, you are deceived, concealed, you escape observation, you are ignored, you will be lost, you are bad and evil and doomed to crawl the underside of the world like a worm. Robert ceased his familiar speculations. Things, he thought, were looking up, and the thought occurred to him literally, namely, in the sense that failure, having always advanced upon him from below, so to speak, must therefore be perpetually gazing up at him. He sat down, his thought echoing all around him, and wondered if he'd been hearing things or if madness were at play once again. His head began to ache. He recalled his doctor's words after the bouts of headaches he used to get: You are a *Luftmensch*, your head is always up in the clouds, that's why you get these headaches. Robert had denied the premise. My feet are firmly planted on the ground. Yes, the doctor argued, but your head is stuck up there in the sky, your whole body is terribly overstretched, affecting your spine, which in turn affects your nervous system. Robert gave a passing thought to the weather in general, wondering if there indeed lay the cause of his headaches, but suspected the doctor of being a quack. The same suspicion had occurred to him once before, when he complained of eye trouble and the healer advised him to refrain from looking at things for a while. No, certainly not, said the doctor, dismissing the weather theory, although it may be a contributory factor aggravating the condition, especially those spiralling frontal systems. When a weather front approaches, he explained, your head is liable to expand or contract, depending on *whether* (here he smiled inanely) we're talking about a low or a high pressure system. Robert acknowledged his pathetic pun with a dour grin, remaining painfully aware that it did nothing to humour him, much less to quell his headaches, and only reinforced his initial suspicions about the man's intelligence and competence. Besides, continued the doctor, backtracking in his diagnosis, your feet set on the ground makes no difference to your head floating among the clouds. What's that got to do with anything? asked Robert. To which the doctor responded with the suggestion that Robert get a job as a weather forecaster: You're a walking weathervane, with a barometer for brains, so you might as well make use of the gifts nature has bestowed on you instead of moping all day long and clasping your head in despair. At which point, as he recalled, Robert would have liked to shoot him, but as he had no gun he couldn't, and didn't. Instead he kissed him on the mouth, passionately and probably out of frustration from not owning a gun. Whereupon the doctor warned him against smoking. Smoking kills, he said. Whom? thought Robert. This thought often came back to him, although he was not a smoker (but for the occasional cigar) and had only indulged in the habit later in life as a social concession to his peers. But the thought on smoking, and the sense of isolation it used to elicit whenever he mixed with smoking friends, reminded him that his acquired habit had served to satisfy a profound communal yearning in his soul, and that his life at that time had frequently attained moments of blissful satisfaction which had previously been denied him. Or was the thought merely a pretext for nostalgia? Hence the fast kiss, which sprang out of uncertainty and confusion, or perhaps out of protest, or for another, deeper reason, and he began to feel a madness buzzing round his head. A childish way of resolving things, he confided to himself, but then Robert was not very old at the time, certainly not half as old as when he had his thought and sat down, when he was old enough, he realised, staring blankly into the snow, to be concerned about ever getting up again. So he got up again in order to allay his new fears. Of course he was old enough to have been retired (though retired from *what* he couldn't say) from a relatively young age. Indeed after retiring from everything (more or less) at an early age, he set himself up in business ("entertainment" he called it when anyone probed too deeply), though his venture collapsed almost as soon as it was launched and forced him to take the bold managerial step of making himself redundant and retiring without so much as a copper handshake. That's how it came about that Robert dabbled in films, which were anything but entertaining. As a cineaste he had aspired to invent "dream-transformations on large rectangular screens for an audience huddled in semi-darkness." Such transformations would be "enormous silent images inscribed in our communal mind." But his business partners distanced themselves from what they regarded as subversive, esoteric ideas, and thought it better for him to pursue such dreams privately in his spare time. They had hoped for far greater things from him, public spectacles in the best Hollywood tradition, but it was not to be and the whole enterprise collapsed. The money people had cut their losses and the episode was quickly forgotten. Rumour had it that Robert, like Robert Walser the writer, had visions that were peculiar to the silent film era, and when he saw how closely attuned these were to his own thoughts, that is, to his notion of thought as pure form circling in his head, he sat down again and reconsidered the problem afresh. In fact he wondered if his retirement from the entertainment business might have been premature, and if therefore his death might have been temporarily, if inadvertently, dropped from the agenda of the living. It occurred to him that his apparently contented disposition with regard to being a failure was showing signs of wear and tear, and he thought that something ought to be done about that. Madness was always lurking at the back of his mind, but for the time being he held back on that option (if that is what it was) as too easy, particularly at his age, and what's more, too fallible a route to success, that is, the success of being totally out of this world, irrevocably exiled in one's madness. Perhaps later in life, when strolling in the snow at dusk, too old to distinguish between madness and the hazard of a little backward step over an open grave, perhaps then he might consider delving into the madness business properly. Or perhaps, he laughed to himself, madness as a form of afterlife, later, as a postscript to life and death, when I'll have all the time in the world to be as mad as I like. Unless, he stopped to reflect briefly as he gazed into the doctor's eyes, time's distractions have a cumulative effect. Are such cumulative effects palpable now? he asked. He grew dizzy as he chased the thought round his head, accompanied by a faintly audible music, then fell into a swoon, leapfrogging the entire century in which his life was lived outside time. Exhausted, he felt he had outlived himself. In a flash he thought of it all as yet another film, set in the mountains, shot in cinemascope format.

＊＊＊

If the film is being made by Robert Walser, dead, then doubt jostles every frame. The unsteady picture is not caused by his hand, but by a trembling heart. Nor is Robert Walser, the Swiss writer, lying expired in the snow, but another with the same name, the same occupation, the same passport. How coincidences occupy the story, and how nothing is to be done about it, will be told. Lenz (another, not the protagonist in George Büchner's tale) wanders in the mountains. A prophet looks on from a nearby summit, caressing his beard and laughing to himself. On the face of it Robert's active corpse creates a philosophical problem. Undoubtedly it is a corpse. Robert, dead, is not merely dying. But it is as plain as the snow on the ground that it is he, not the other, making the film. We long for concrete explanations but none are forthcoming. I have been writing for three hours. Now I'm tired. I'd rather be out in the sunshine. Soon I'll quit, go out, enjoy the sun. But I remind myself that too much sun gives me headaches. Unless in winter, when (ironically) excessive cold has the same effect, while the sun (when it penetrates the cloudcover) more or less palliates the bitterness. Because I can't tolerate too much sun (in spring or in summer) I wish the good life for those who deserve it. Not for myself, certainly. The good life, what we know of it in the madhouse, is a tortuous haul on the byways of boredom and only an added torment for active corpses. Still, I'd like to relax within my own death, become tangential to my own existence and possibly be in a position to extricate my corporeality from the mechanics of the situation. I would consider being dead were it not for the traumatic ordeal of funerals, the bitter recriminations and regrets among survivors, the grotesque carnival of maggots and worms crawling into dead flesh, etc. Even my own projected apprehensions are a fair consideration for delaying death, as if afterthoughts could be articulated in that quagmire of nothingness. And yet some experts maintain that whereas film is a collaborative process, death is a conspiracy in which everyone but the dead participates. But I find this line of thought untenable, since in such a conspiracy the conspirators could only be among the dead, their allegiances as clearly defined as gravestones under the light of a full moon. So perhaps there is an angel of death after all, a celestial gofer dealing with the mundane affairs of dying without disclosing his status to the world. No doubt his position would be privileged, if somewhat sterile, being neither living nor dead, the butt of humour at best or a pretext for evil at worst. On the other hand, perhaps we simply do not possess the faculty of apprehending death when it sings (or stings) us. We speak of the disposal of corpses as if they comprised material evidence against the living (as they do, of course) but such talk implicates our language in that conspiracy. As far as I can see there is no way of getting round it without resorting to incantations, prayers, blessings, curses or similar devices. In that respect the soul is merely an ancient contraption (like a hot-air balloon) for bearing common psychological disorders such as fear of flying or anorexia. The discovery of the soul is apocryphal, after all, and specious claims have been made on its behalf. It is the pennant hoisted daily from the anti-death camp, and although it beguiles us with its seductive fluttering, like some angel dancing among the stars, it can't begin to touch the corporeality of a dying writer collapsed in snow. I am not a materialist. Far from it. But when I describe the process of Robert making the film, his work with light and shadow, words become entangled in a morass of images like a clump of snarled wires trapped in the mind. It is then that discrepancies arise, like those between images glimpsed in dreams and garbled sounds produced in sleep. When we discover these things upon waking, death already grips us with its immovable black gaze. So we don't flinch, we don't twitch, we dare not even pick up a pen out of fear – we simply die.

At noon I caught myself in the act of writing, moments after I had said I would cease. Not that I lied about the sun, about being in it. I did go into the sun, but by writing in it I've compromised myself as well as the sun. The sun is not to be written in, and writing is not to be glared at by sunlight or warmed by its rays. The sun in a cloudless sky in late spring or early summer in a high latitude country makes for hot weather. I've taken off my shirt and can feel the sun's radiation needling my skin. There are those who would describe today's weather as perfect. No doubt they've set their sights low and would consider themselves (in this garden, on this blissful spring day) happy souls! They are unlikely to take into account what may or may not happen next. For example, the plane banks sharply to the left – East, I believe. This claustrophobic flight of fancy in my head will be the death of me, a sudden chill, a false sound in the air will suffice. The plane will explode in mid-air, as it has on a previous trip. Like the Second Exile this second death in a mid-air explosion is part of a series of recurrent phenomena which social scientists have dubbed the Turnstile Effect. There are psychologists who have deliber- ately lost their minds in search of its cause. I know they were not looking for me. I had nothing to do with it. Now it's moving, the sun. The sun edging carefully behind a tree, as if to hide. But this is patently wrong. It is I who should be moving, I who should make the effort of taking a few paces left or right if I want to keep in line with the sun's position, that is, if I want to be caressed by its beams and keep away from the tree's shade. I have an obliga- tion to stay on my toes in this perpetual cosmological dance. So I ask myself if my moving would be worth the effort, but in posing the question I lose the thread of the dance. I'm reduced to a pathetic figure so badly in need of a little sunshine that for all his effort his reason collapses under the pale weight of encroaching shadows. Rather than move I ask questions. Do I really need to keep in line with the sun's rays and, given that I do, given that this is a kind of life-support system, how long and at what speed would I need to move around this garden, this country, this entire globe, in order to accomplish the task? (Success here is an ogre hiding behind an oven door – an unlikely figure of paternal trust.) I calculate quietly, doggedly, like a dumb detective with nothing to do, for no-one has died recently under any suspicious circumstances and these days old writers are prone to dropping dead in snow. And suddenly it's night, falling like a veil, a hammer, a dark pall, a calendar leaf, a cloud of amnesia, or a litany of phrases and invocations oscillating between a frail 'yes' and a petrified 'no'. It can't be the birds singing, I'm told. It can't be a choir of angels. It must be all in my head, they say.

***

Not feeling in the least dead, I have a dream in which I'm sleeping. I undergo it rather than have it, for the dream is not my possession and whatever I say about it is clouded by a fog which sleep casts over me. Within the dream reality is circumscribed by an icy flame, a sensation of eternal heat which I cannot exorcise with words and which leaves me half-frozen with exasperation. A flame without fire, a flickering of perpetual light and heat. Restlessly I awake without opening my eyes. Heidi arrives and straddles my lap. She presses hard kisses on my eyelids as the plane banks to the left – East, I believe. An ache generates behind my eyelids, which I can neither open nor shut, and a voice warns me not to dismiss this as a dream: It is not a dream. It is probably the voice of a father, though this is a conjecture which needs to be substantiated in a more objective manner. Then the plane explodes in mid-air. A utopian gesture of a finger eased deep into the clouds' core lingers in the back of my mind, while God sighs in a whirlwind that reverberates in the sky. The little pillow behind my head is ablaze. The flame creeps into my ear, warm and wet and blinding, singeing my nerve-ends as it licks its way into my brain. My legs have blown away in the disaster, leaving two stumps bleeding with an incurable homesickness. The malady affects my body with bouts of seizure which may, according to the flight doctor, cause headaches which in turn could lead to heart failure. I am about to say something, about to express my feelings, maybe sing or something of that kind, but the doctor tells me the time's up. It's time, he says, jotting down something on a scrap of paper. I never understand what he means – nor would he ever notice my incomprehension, for whenever he tolls in that officious way I leave the room instantly, and he never complains. He always seems happy about it and I always return for more.

***

The doctor seems to be suggesting that I take a permanent vacation. He doesn't spell it out in so many words but gives me the gist. Go away, don't bother me with the madness business in your head, he seems to be saying. Just go die quietly in a faraway country, he'd like to say. In fact he sometimes articulates those very words but pretends they just slipped out or were intended for another Robert. As there is no other Robert in the room I find this hard to believe. I remind him that we live in a shrinking world and no place would really be far enough. Even as I leave he seems to be sighing with relief, mumbling subdued phrases which sound like prayers offered up to God in thanks. I presume he's thanking God for his deliverance from me. If so, it's a curious response, since we're both perfectly aware that his reprieve is only temporary, that I'll be back the following day for my usual appointment or sooner if something urgent comes up overnight. Personally I have no faith in medicine, and unfortunately (for me) the doctor has already sussed this out. It's really because of a guilty social conscience that I visit him at all, not for any pressing medical reasons, though he's not aware of this, nor would he appreciate it if he was. I have the usual medical complaints, of course, but they're secondary compared to my concern over his social welfare. I generally worry over the unemployment rate among professionals, and when such professionals are those with whom I have a personal relationship, my anxiety is all the greater. In my own small way I try to help society, and so from time to time pay the doctor a visit. Whether I visit by appointment or on the off-chance, whether on a daily, weekly or monthly basis, all this is irrelevant. I mention it only because I'm frequently asked (not just by the doctor but by his staff and by total strangers who write to me from various municipal offices) why I need to see the doctor so frequently. It's not easy to lie in such circumstances, and I'm usually forced to invent a little white lie so as not to compromise him, or indeed myself. It's easy to see that the last thing someone like me needs, someone who is always off on a tangent, ducking into the nearest available digression in order to protect the reputation of others, is to break off from his routine and visit the doctor. I say it again, it's only my guilt-ridden conscience that drives me there, not some indeterminable hankering for a panacea or the desperate need for company. So when he offered his diagnosis I was flabbergasted. In fact I took exception to it. I need constancy, I told him, not rest. That's when I kissed him, and that's when he lectured me on smoking and the mortality rate, his euthanasic eyes gleaming like stainless steel needles. And that's when I left. The birds in this garden, their sweet chirping, that is, never cease to amaze me. Politely I mention their song to the doctor, who accuses me of digressing and avoiding the issue. I refer him to Keats at midnight, hearing a nightingale. I explain to the doctor that it could only have been a nightingale or an owl – what other nocturnal birds sing around here? As the difference between them is unmistakable, you couldn't really go wrong in naming either one. It's not like trying to differentiate from among the hundreds of species chirping simultaneously in a chaotic din, as in this garden at this moment. Apart from the chorus of birds, there's the distant drone of cars and trains, and the occasional crescendo of a plane taking off above me – heading East, no doubt. All of which is as confusing to me as it never was to Keats. The doctor advises me to take aspirins when I leave the country. It will clear your headaches and help to counteract the nicotine in your blood, he says. Waving, he adds: good-bye.

***

Occasionally, when the streets are quiet late at night or early in the morning, I talk to myself. Once, on my way back from the doctor's, I said: I'm in two minds about it. I've always been in two minds about it and will always remain in two minds about it. It is infinitely better than being completely mindless about it and at least marginally better than being in many (say, one hundred) minds about it. Being in two minds is generally better than being totally confused about the problem, which is: should I be examined and diagnosed by a doctor if I feel healthy but am beginning to show signs of illness, or do I let nature take its course and see how things develop? I stopped a lonely pedestrian and asked if these signs of illness aren't "natural" at my age, especially (I explained to the bewildered dog-walker) for someone who has lived the kind of life that I have. My interlocutor nodded uncertainly. I did not want to press her, but the fact is I couldn't understand if she was nodding 'Yes' or offering a tentative 'No' by shaking her fine head. I was talking about mental, not physical, illness, but there was no time to explain. She seemed to be in a hurry and presumed I was mad. At what time in our lives (this was the crucial question, though she never heard it properly) do we tell ourselves what we would rather not hear? When do we break the taboo, I asked, and say to ourselves enough is enough, or enough is insufficient, or less than a surfeit? Even as I formulated the question I could hear its endless permutations fading out of earshot with the lady's footsteps. These days the two minds in which I consider the problem are diametrically opposed: when one says "never," the other says "always." Sometimes I have a way of resuscitating my dead problems. Nor is it just a question of *when*, but of *what* it is that should or should not be said once we know when to say it. Since all this is widely known but rarely mentioned, "what" becomes the given element in a familiar equation, whilst the "when" of it becomes a quantifiable unknown which remains hidden yet soluble, looming like an enticing X on a blank page, much in the way that *Madam X* invites a viewing of a film by that name, in which the mysterious woman may or may not appease our violent expectations. Perhaps I'm a criminal at large whose anonymity depends upon his own ignorance about the crime. As a rule I do not talk to strangers, for fear of learning things spontaneously. I mean incriminating things about myself. I've confessed a number of dubious deeds to the authorities, but none of these have qualified as crimes. I can only deduce from this that my language must be lagging behind the events that conspire to describe my life. Simple guesswork is inadequate if we want to apportion guilt justly. Scientific experiments have shown that guilt can only be mediated through a genetic route. In most cases this means that it settles into our consciousness some hundreds of generations after the event, when it may be fairly or unfairly carried about by someone like myself, for instance, or the beautiful woman with the dog. I thought of Abraham and his son and wondered what the streets were like late at night or early in the morning in those days, whether anyone saw anything suspicious and, as it seems more than likely that someone did, why they failed to prevent the attempted act which ultimately led to my terrible guilt. I believe the lady with the dog was withholding information about that traumatic ordeal, which explains why she rushed off so quickly. She had the bearing of someone who could keep a secret for a long time. But it's futile dreaming about it and tormenting ourselves with the endless possibilities of its consequences. As soon as the traffic picks up and the streets become active again we put ourselves on alert and struggle like animals to keep out of harm's way. I'll vouch for that personally, for I was almost hit by a car once on my way to the doctor's, simply because I failed to take heed as darkness descended around my speech.

***

There are regulations we have to abide by in this madhouse. If, for example, one of us imagines himself to be Moses, there must be another who can claim to be Aaron. This simple logic dictates our fate. Lunch is between 12:30 and 1PM. Dinner is at 6:45PM. Breakfast is at 8:00AM. We do our activities in pairs (a buddy system as in summer camp) and each of us is allocated a partner, so that we bear responsibility for our own as well as our partner's safety. For example, Jesus is coupled with John the Baptist, who sometimes cross-dresses as Mary. Our behaviour seems non-conformist on the surface, but in fact it is in strict conformity with the majority of textbook cases – how else would we be authorised to be mad? When it comes to choosing a character we have considerable freedom, though in fact the characters are bequeathed to us before we're fully conscious of having made our choice. Who bequeaths them is not something that concerns us – after all, we are in a madhouse, not in a summer camp. To an outsider our personality disorders may seem self-evident, so that it's only natural for Moses to be paired with Aaron, for Jesus to seek out Mary, and so on. But if the outsider looked closely, he would see that the degree of conviction which each of us carries within himself is dependent on some sinister goings-on under the surface. What sinister goings-on? Well, every morning the doctor has a brief chat with each of us lunatics before we wander off into our little worlds. Afterwards he makes notes in his book. It seems he is tracking our progress, charting our position, so to speak, like a navigator following dots on a screen that tell him about the course of a spaceship heading for a distant galaxy. Your personality is a passport in which every movement is recorded, and every entrance and exit stamped. It is carefully scrutinised before they let you into this part of the world, especially if your behaviour is somewhat abnormal. We know all this in advance, like the familiar pattern of the night sky, but we cannot be sure what it means until our spaceship has already blasted off. Earlier we were saying: We are in the mountains. We dogs friendly to Diogenes are wagging our tails because Robert Walser has finally risen from the snow and is directing his film about Lenz. Arnold Schoenberg has now descended the Venusberg to conduct his *Accompaniment to a Film Scene*. The scene calls for the characters to come together and fall asunder again in a single frame, in $1/24^{th}$ of a second. The scene also has Lenz continuing to brood prophetically over his own fate. Lenz, the actor, meanwhile, rather selfishly ignores Robert's difficulties with the script. It is the same old story, he says, of eternal conflict between Man and God, between Yes and No and Maybe, and the crew, the cast and the orchestra have been obsessively preoccupied with it during the course of Robert's lifetime. Like Robert Walser, he sighs for the lack of strength with which to laugh. When it comes to dying, the great humanist tradition stands in the corner of the room, along with other mourners paying their last respects. Like all late arrivals, its gesture is silent, its modesty futile.

He called his childhood memories 'inventions' and shared them with me in his own words whenever we played. Like the psychiatrist who liked to nod beside him as he spoke, I nodded acquiescently much of the time. Occasionally I uttered "ehm" or "oh" or "ah", but mostly I maintained a disciplined silence. At times I had to suppress the urge to respond verbally to those emotional descriptions. During such hermetic moments I found my dumbness couched in a curious swooning sensation of a religious magnitude. I deduced from this that I may have been a Trappist monk in a previous life. The order in which I've chosen to re-tell these things is that of his own narration rather than their true chronological order or that in which Robert has spontaneously re-arranged his memories in his mind. I believe it is less important to know precisely what came when than what his inventions actually were and how they materialised in a particular context. He reminded me that his auto-narration was not synchronous with any objective historical reality and that his family's various anecdotes, recorded in different ledgers at different times, would be at odds with his own recollections of his childhood wanderings. As far as I was concerned this was perfectly acceptable. He conceded that at times his mind had strayed too far, further than his body would have allowed had it been in control. But he claimed that as he was not a dualist, this discrepancy never affected him; he said it was just a minor aberration, like snowflakes in the middle of June.

A night view through the porthole of a second-class cabin on board a ship sailing West from the Holy Land. Noises skim the surface of the blackened sea as the ship stops off the Cypriot coast to take on passengers from a launch. The island's distant scattered lights converge like star-clusters within the circumference of the window. Nothing else to be seen, but a sense of drama looms, like the exhilaration that grips you when the curtain rises on a familiar tragedy: you can smell the blood even before the first word is spoken. I hear the boat's sputtering engine and the ship's gangway knocking against the hull, a chaotic overlay of mechanical noises punctuated by passengers' cries – hurried, nervous voices in an unfamiliar language. Other mysterious sounds rise to my ears from the stillness of the water, but, as in a dream, there is no recourse to a reply. Disparate voices coalesce as if their sun had anchored in midnight, its fruit black. The adventure is confounded by trepidation in my heart. The night is interminable, a midnight seized in its tracks. My mother frets, worrying about the domestic arrangements in the cabin, the basin with those funny unworkable taps. Europe begins to feel ominous, its grandeur mingling in the air with diesel fumes and soot particles settling on the flimsy lace curtain around the window. Outside, in the dark, standing bodies rock on the water, heaving their ancient luggage on board with a thud.

***

An act of madness borne out of absence, or surfeit, of love – how can I be sure? Heidi is a misnomer if we're speaking of love, a label with comic overtones, sentimental fringes, tassels, ear-locks and a thousand loose appendages draping the body of love. I

80

writhe as I write: *Dear H...*, expelling the breath that holds her body within its name. The name a greeting, a virtual embrace between angels. I wring out my life in its absence. The body hidden, glimpsed as melody inside a lunatic's mind, watching and waiting above, in the sky, at dusk or at night, star-filled, with a crescent moonbeam's slurred speech marking time. A figure holding the body (romantic, red, blazing forth out of a pale sky) steps onto a wide screen: bright illuminated shadow, passing imperceptibly from view like a soul going from life to death, or vice versa – who's to say? These things can't be accurately measured nor reliably witnessed. His longing – intangible, invisible, behind the camera, not in front – is only the possibility of a neglect of pain. We can't be sure. And the pain yielding the body of love is a first lesson in time, an anthem without words which we memorise. While Heidi sleeps, I sleep. It is the waking moment that incites me to act. Out of madness, in compliance with madness, I obey the laws of our madhouse. What am I saying? I'm giving the game away. Do I retract his suffering, expose his heavenly landscape, let the angels copulate in the clouds? On deck, shortly after sunset between Piraeus and Naples, I vomit, giving all to the sea but the pain – my head buried in her breasts, giddy and senseless head gasping traces of Swiss air – or was it perfume? An air coming off the sea, bearing small scattered snowflakes in its ethereal spume, a hint of Alps playing in the mind. She will say that the sun melts snow in summer there, while in winter it lies plain like a sheet – sometimes slightly ruffled by the imprint of a fallen body.

***

I was surprised to receive a personal communication from Lenz. As I read through it I realised that the Lenz in question was not George Büchner's hero but the pseudo-actor in Robert's film. Significantly, Robert has never mentioned him. My surprise was all the greater as the content of his confession seemed so familiar, even predictable, the more I read of it. From the information at my disposal I assumed that Lenz's relationship with Robert (dead or alive) was filial, though even in such a clear-cut case we cannot be absolutely sure who is playing the father, who is playing the son – indeed how much of it is play and how much of it is real. I hope you do not object to this interpolation of Lenz's letter into Robert's inventions. Even if my hypothesis proves false, I feel morally obliged to include it here. And so I offer it humbly, with the sensitivity that it demands and an acute awareness of its pertinence to Robert's posthumous inventions.

"Dear H: Your questionnaire on the nature of my difficulties and my present condition draws me into a brief story of my life, enclosed in this letter." *(I was baffled by this obscure reference, as this was the first and only communication I'd ever had with him and I had no idea what questionnaire he was talking about.)* "I am depressed. I find it difficult to focus for any length of time on any particular project, although there are days when that difficulty somehow disappears, as if by magic. I've often been depressed in the past, melancholic, though I'm not sure what the difference is, but I've usually found a way to alleviate depression through work.

I'm an actor and, like most actors, am usually without work, which only exacerbates the problem. Whilst my work has some therapeutic value (as work often has) it does not offer me a forum for my psychological problems. But recently it has tended in that direction and I find such a tendency boring, narcissistic and frustrating. I say 'boring' yet wonder if the word does not conceal a sense of shame, evoking the stigma of mental illness in a society ruled by an ideology of the body and a crude work ethic. My problem is that I can't break away from that self-obsessive trend, which affects my daily life more radically now than ever before. I know of actors who have been 'suicided by society', like Antonin Artaud, who first died as Marat stabbed in his bath, with eyes rolled up imploring God. I have no intention of joining that club. More recently the director dropped dead in the snow while making a film in which I was to play the leading role – dropped, that is, in a wilful sort of way, as when people fall on their knees to pray; as he fell he failed to acknowledge my presence, his protégé and in some ways his son. These things happen, I know. Perhaps he was out of his mind by then. Yet I too propel myself in the same direction as those who have been or would be 'suicided', nurturing every opportunity to sink deeper into a mad hopelessness. When I think about it rationally, I recognise the need to pick myself up, have another go (or should it be *stab*?) at living, but the source of energy which I used to draw upon in the past seems to have dissipated in this thin Alpine air. But my request for help is tentative. I have serious reservations about following up psychiatric advice and being drawn into the madness business. As an artist I feel threatened by the prospect of therapy. To allow myself that indulgence would be to sanction the violation of my own domain, to let my thinking be encroached upon and manipulated by representatives from that circle of understanders, gurus of the soul, medicine men with elbow patches on their jackets instead of medicine in their cupboards. Worst of all, it would mean submitting my voice, the wellspring of my art, to a process which is not only antithetical to it but blatantly antagonistic towards it. I am aware that this kind of rationalisation may be interpreted as a smoke-screen to hide the truth about myself. As a rational being I can appreciate the need for acknowledging defects in my personality, the psychic wounds that show up through the mask, blah blah. But I am not an actor by accident. Even if I concede that necessity, I would still argue against it on the grounds that it is the responsibility of art to deal with the truths about ourselves and the world we live in. As an artist I accept that responsibility unequivocally. Then why – I hear you echoing my own questions – why hire a psychiater? Why bother with a shrinkomat?" *(I found his use of the term 'psychiater' disturbingly quaint and rather pretentious. On the other hand, I was amused by the inventive twist he gave to the idea of cleansing, where the neologism 'shrinkomat' seemed to be modelled on 'laundromat,' neatly incorporating the economical concept of pay-as-you-wash.)* "Psychoanalysis and Art have long been at war with each other, an undeclared war – in fact, an ice cold war in search of a spark. The peace between them has not come through co-existence but through a mutual suspicion, fostered by the power of illusion. Each side has waged a campaign of contempt, nourished by the deep desire for each other's annihilation and cultural extinction. Even so, I hear a small liberal voice inside me rejecting my own doubt and offering a caveat that invokes the simple criterion of objectivity, something we artists preen ourselves with occasionally. It tells me to look at things from another point of view, to cast a more neutral light on the matter, regardless of the merits or defects of such a view. Oh, how I despise that rationalistic voice. It knows only how to meddle in things. It has the effect of making me look like a buffoon, a grotesque totalitarian visionary with cheap makeup. At times this image has haunted me on stage or in front of the camera. Consequently, yes, there is a case to be made for seeking help, even if (as I believe) such help is completely futile. Now with regard to your question on separations – yes, there have been a few, the first of course being the expulsion from the womb, or birth, what you would call the Primal Exile. (Forgive me, I've been perusing your books.) Other separations have invariably involved a conflation of people and places in various places and times, notably during the Second Exile, when the Temple was destroyed and our family fled East. More recently, Robert's death in the snow was our separation from life (obviously), yet without so much as a wave of the hand. The tragic event has been, I know, the catalyst for my depressive mood, but the underlying causes are deeply rooted and I have been conscious of them for most of my life. Once we travelled to Berlin – or Hamburg. I was too young, my thoughts always with Heidi, and had no idea where the Alps were. We had to leave our dog behind to guard the Holy Land. A small mutt, he died soon after our departure (our separation, as you would say) from an ear infection. Then of course there was the separation between Heidi and her mother, precipitated by her parents' separation – through death, I believe. Because we visited Germany we also visited Brussels, where Heidi's mother lived, and saw the Great Atom at the World Fair. At the time I had not been informed of the splitting of the atom – a separation from itself, as you would say – which happened long before our visit, though I was made vaguely aware of a city named Hiroshima, and of events which came to be called the Holocaust, and of other catastrophes beginning with H. Another separation that comes to mind, while I'm on the subject, is that of Heidi's finger from her hand – that is, the top of her ring finger was missing, from a childhood accident with a kitchen knife, I believe. This half-digit for me was the heart of her sex, its semi-absence not a deformity but a stark revelation. Since then I've meditated on the little death of her finger and have come to realise that she could never marry anyone but me. This passion for Heidi was not an innocent childhood infatuation. I don't know what you would call it, but the severance of her finger from herself was the promise of our bondage, as if every scribbled line I make were an object she could touch. And if you were to write to her even now, in her old age, she would corroborate these things with a smile."

It was at this point that my suspicions about Lenz's real identity came to the fore and, as confirmed to me later on in Robert's inventions, seemed justified. It was in fact Robert himself who had assumed the role of Lenz all along, not only in the guise of the actor but also as the Lenz with the dual aspects, historical and fictional, in Büchner's story. Later I learned that Robert suffered from a common personality disorder and that each of the characters he mentioned, from Diogenes and his dogs to Heidi and the beautiful woman in the street, was a part of his own personality, quite literally figments of his imagination. I suppose I should have been alerted to the problem much earlier than I was, in fact when he used to refer to himself as a corpse, which at the time I mistook for a simple metaphor of his life. At any rate the following fragments were detected underneath the writing of his 'Lenz' letter, a palimpsest that only became apparent once the 'Lenz' ink began to fade. His inventions, on the other hand, continued to come into being in their usual spontaneous manner and he submitted them to my attention as we played.

Ethics

When I enjoy this concurrent suffering, just as I would my death-as-suffering, I am made aware of not yet having said it and, almost thinking it, of lapsing into the madness of its pain. I say it only when the words I use to enunciate it explode in contradictions. It is here that meaning achieves its non-existence in a blinding light, as they say. I enjoy my suffering and suffer my madness. There is no sense in all of it, only a faint pulsating rhythm in some indefinable region of the brain, maybe somewhere beside or under the brain altogether, like a chunk of thought falling in outer space.

[.....]

West out of the Holy Land – "The Nazis, you know who they were...?" was the standard rhetorical question – we sail to the Holocaust Land. My mother is pining for her youth, her childhood, and dreams that the whole final solution had never been proposed. The politics of it all was as remote from her consciousness as the poetry of Hölderlin, though the event tore everyone's minds to pieces as if they'd been set upon by Maenads at the moment of illumination – in the glare of deliverance. The ship docks at Marseilles. We traverse a city where, in a shop-window, a wooden box with a pale olive-green glass front promises visions from afar of real people and real things. We board a train at Gare

du... and then head North through tunnels and picture-book landscapes. Dusk is always falling; persistent. Düsseldorf is always
approaching; Heidi always waiting. The damp cobblestones, the
grey houses, the well-articulated German accents over the footsteps on the pavements – this is her boudoir and its million objects. I can smell her skin.

[.....]

Ethics

In order to improve, I re-write. I make a conscious effort to steer
for a truth and a poem. I hope these are not contradictory forces.
Have been generally mentally healthy and have had no history of
mental illness. The facts are contradictory, it seems. When signs
of mental illness show themselves I dabble in its treatment with a
natural home-grown remedy. This often instigates a piece of writing, sometimes a little film. If the latter, then Diogenes appears
as an extra with the aura of a star. My therapeutic dabbling has
always had the nature of a preventative measure rather than a
cure. To make art is to present. The joy or pain derived from the
thing presented is merely a side-effect. Ironically another side-
effect of my obsession with art is that it keeps madness temporarily at bay. The bay of madness, where a pair of lovers can be
seen bobbing in a row-boat, is also known as the sanatorium.
Preoccupied with the re-write, I see the consequent failures looming – not like clouds but like massive blank walls threatening to
collapse. Despite stringent building regulations, the sanatorium's

walls are made of paper. Which is where I am at the moment, facing them with a dumb gaze whichever way I turn.

EXT – DAY

It is a good morning. Dawn light creeps in over the hills. Birds break the night's leftover silence.

The sanatorium is waking up: three or four small buildings around a courtyard, where patients with nothing to do go about their business with uncharacteristic cheerfulness. One by one the lights go out in the windows, doors bang open and shut, groggy voices exchange greetings in the dimness.

A white-coated orderly emerges from the main building after his night shift. He gets on his bike and cycles through the courtyard, calling out "Good morning!" to a group of patients.

One of the patients responds: "It is a good morning, Mr Hielfer. Today we're not just going to be madmen, we're going to do something. We're going to act madmen!"

"That shouldn't be too difficult," he shouts back, continuing on his way.

[Robert Walser is directing a film called Lenz, for which he uses his fellow patients as cast and crew. They go off to a nearby hillside to shoot a scene. On the other side of the hill, just over the crest, an orchestra made up of musical patients plays Schoenberg's *Accompaniment to a Film Scene.* The music chases away the birds, then flies in their pursuit.

Walser takes Lenz to one side and explains: "People don't want to be reminded – they want to be shocked. Your job is to shock them without acting. People don't want actors, they want models into which they can pour their own emotions." Lenz, actor and main character, nods agreeably. He has understood. The police are making a documentary about Walser's filming, for which they will provide their own commentary.]

[.....]

Once I saw him standing outside. He placed his head in his hands as if it were a foreign object, concealing it. His hands grew large and a darkness enveloped his head in a kind of deep oozing fluid. A hum from the depth of his throat rocked him back and forth in a movement of supplication; he looked like a nun hiding inside her husband's wound. Three times his hands covered his face and three times he gaped into the darkness. The window through which I observed him was shut and I could only hear my own breathing. There was no time to act, as in an emergency, only to reflect. I reflected that I must have felt the vibrations of his hum without hearing its sound. I drew the curtains and waited for his arrival. As we played I said nothing about his gaping into the wound and he too let the matter rest, as though it had been mere conjecture, an hallucination of my silence.

(Heidi's skin was not singed by the Nazis. As Robert lay in the snow, all but dead, he remembered lucidly how her skin was not burned. Like Robert Schumann, he began to see things that were not there, feeling them, tactile yet absent phantoms that came into being randomly and vanished with the same lightness of touch. Then Heidi placed her skin against his face....) At the moment of his death Robert did not believe that life went on, but that it stopped – and he found it impossible to cry and to die at the same time.

photo by Adi Hollander

GAD HOLLANDER's books are: *The Palaver* (Book Works, London 1998), with visual work by Andrew Bick, *Sleep, Memory* (New Pyramid Press, London 1988) and *Figures of Speech* (edition fundamental, Cologne 1987). His work has appeared in the literary journals *Curtains, Central Park, Acts, Temblor, Reality Studios, Paper Air* and *First Intensity*. He has also directed the films/videos *Diary of a Sane Man* (1990), shown at Berlin Film Festival & broadcast on Channel 4 (UK); *Euripides' Movies* (1987); *Background Music (Orphic)* (1986) and *Mnemosyne* (1985). He lives in London, was born in Jerusalem and spent (in/un-) formative years in Queens, New York.